ART OF A DEAL WITH THE DEVIL

ART OF A DEAL WITH THE DEVIL

Percy Twenty-Five Brown
& Ruby Brown

ISBN: 979-8-89465-057-9 (sc)
ISBN: 979-8-89465-058-6 (e)

Integrity Publishing
39343 Harbor Hills Blvd Lady Lake,
FL 32159

www.integrity-publishing.com

"You know, I'm thinking about something that I studied in school. One of my favorite subjects was Anthropology. I was especially interested when Anthropology classes examined religion, magic and witchcraft. One of my most exciting assignments was researching cases that involve witchcraft and selling one's soul to the devil.

It is especially interesting watching news stories which possibly include incidents of people selling their souls. I am reminded of some of my case studies when I read about occurrences that have some similarity to those cases.

Before my studies in Anthropology, I believed in a spiritual world. (My mom forced me to go to church.) In church I learned to fear GOD and the devil. I feared and avoided spiritual stuff but, sometimes you encounter things you cannot find an explanation for. I was more than excited when I learned about Anthropology.

In some of the cases I studied, strange and sometimes unexplainable incidents occurred with people accused of associations with the devil. One could conclude that it is possible to make deals with dark spirits.

I think of this when I hear of popular and successful entertainers dying young or under unusual circumstances. These cases cause me to remember some of the facts in the cases I studied in Anthropology. I find myself wondering if that person sold his soul for fame and fortune, without realizing that time passes quickly and the "payment due" date always comes too soon.

I found myself explaining to my wife that, I am almost convinced that I am watching one of these cases in progress. Although these are my own thoughts and opinions, look how the pieces fall into place so beautifully. I asked my wife to consider this scenario. If a smart man (smart in his own mind) decided that he could get his desires by selling his soul to the devil and be brave enough to do it, he may find that there is a lot more to this belief than he thought.

His desires may materialize faster and more abundantly than he realizes. The person may have been warned that the devil is a 'trickster'. When things are going well, the person gets harder to convince or if he is convinced, he may feel like he can outsmart the devil.

Since he would be getting everything, he would go all the way. He would not be like those "other fools", who sold their souls for just months of fame and fortune. He would be smart enough to get it all. He would not just want fame and fortune. He would want all the fame and all the fortune. He would want to be in the news constantly. Everyone would know him. He would want to be on the list of the richest people in the world. Not only that but be able to "rub shoulders" with the richest and most powerful people in the world.

He would want to have businesses all over the world and the most beautiful women would surround him whenever, wherever he is present. He would want to be able to hold parties and gatherings for the world's richest and most influential people but, more so than anything else, he would want to be able to boast to these people about his greatness. Satan would find that he was not dealing with a "punk", he was dealing with someone who knew something about making deals.

Some do not even consider these types of deals because of fear. However, there are those who have tried. There are stories about how the devil plays tricks on his conquest. Religions warn against and, sometimes give advice on avoiding the devil's tricks. In my studies, I found that the devil always lives up to his descriptions "the trickster, the liar, the deceiver, the accuser, the author of confusion, etc.". He is not your friend and has no interest in fair treatment. He is known to find ways to make your own wishes turn against you (that seems to be entertainment for him). Those who feel that they are too smart for that often find themselves in deep trouble.

My observations have led me to believe that there is a devil and that he does seek out and that he does collect souls. For him it's a game. An art. People can become slaves to their own desires. The devil is an expert at temptation. Why is the soul so valuable that fame, fortune and power can be easily exchanged for it? Those with fame, fortune and power are envied and some without it seem to feel that these people do not have problems. Many of the stories are similar because desires are similar.

I sometimes compare myself to others when I learn of their situations. (I do not consider myself a representative of the average man.) I think I have an advantage. I was born poor and never had any great expectations. I have been homeless, so I feel that just having a roof over my head is a blessing. It does not take a lot to make me happy. I find peace in some of the philosophies that I've learned. My favorite quote is: "A man is rich when he knows that he has enough," (Eastern Philosophy). I find that a peaceful spirit and a satisfied mind are the most valuable things a person can own.

In studying Religion, Magic and Witchcraft, I find that most people believe the same thing. Whether a person is religious or not, there is some idea of good and evil. We also know that sometimes what we feel is good for us is not necessarily good for others. We either respect others or we don't. Again there is an Eastern Philosophy that says, "Those who do not respect enough will not be respected."

What seems to be the most important to some people means nothing to others. I would like to have all my bills paid. I would like to be able to relax and enjoy years with my wife and family. I would like for us to be stress free, healthy, of sound mind and body, and still able to laugh and have fun.

I am past 75 years old. I don't feel like doing things like I used to do. I don't suppose others have the same enthusiasm about doing things as they once did. Holding a position of great power would be too stressful for me. I would not want to be still interested in obtaining other businesses because I would want to have reached a place where I could enjoy the things that I have done until a reasonable time to retire. I have also learned what greed is and what it can do.

I would like to be able to just disappear with my wife sometimes. Just take off and go somewhere without having to report to anyone where we are or why. I would like to be able to just sit back and relax sometimes and not answer the phone and not have to worry that there's something so pressing that it makes a difference. I would like to know that if there is a God and I must be judged He will find that I tried to be a good man.

Making the deal is easy and, in many cases, it is done unwittingly. It usually requires the strength to put aside what you feel is right or correct to do what is necessary to obtain your desires. Having been raised in poverty, I have a clear understanding of why people go out of their way to avoid being poor. Selling the soul involves overriding what you feel is right (hungry children can steal, knowing that it is wrong). There is a clear difference between one who steals because of hunger and one who decides to adopt stealing, lying, cheating and other means to obtain more wealth when they are already considered rich.

The smart deal maker has already decided that he is willing to disregard the laws of God and man to obtain his desires. That person may be surprised at first when he sees that he's gotten away with something the average person would not have. However, after the deal is made, he may find unusual things happening more and more. He may end up telling himself, "I did not expect this" as his fortune and fame grows.

This is the time the person usually finds himself happy that he has made a deal. He can put himself above others and feel the envy of those who are aware of his wealth and power. Problems arise when things don't go exactly the way they were expected to. After a while, the person making the deal with the devil usually finds that there were misunderstandings when the deal was made.

It's not easy getting to a point where you are considered one of the richest people in the world, but it is possible. The problem is, although it is already established that the person understands that lying, cheating, stealing and acts that are considered contrary to good are necessary for his ambitions. He finds that more of these acts are required than he imagined, but necessary to reach his goal. By the time he reaches this understanding it is too late to back out and he does not want to because things are going too well.

There is a feeling that if one becomes powerful enough, he can make the rules. He may even be able to express his disagreements with the devil. Small problems begin to arise. Although they are small, there should not be any problems. It would not be expected that problems could arise from something so trivial as someone saying that "you are not as rich as you say you are".

The dealer may want to become one of the most powerful people in the world. The devil would put him in a powerful position, but for a much shorter time than he ever realized. The power is much more than the person would want to give up and there's never enough time in the position to accomplish all the things the dealer has in mind. It is around this time that the person begins to feel that the devil might be cheating him. The person might be willing to do anything to keep his position but, everything he tries brings more problems and trouble for himself and the devil no longer seems to be answering when he calls for help.

OVERD
FINAL NOTICE
OVER
E
DUE

Being listed with the richest people in the world does not mean a whole lot if you have stress because some do not believe that you are as wealthy as you say you are. The dealer may enlist help from those who he feels have the same mindset as him, but it would eventually be hard to overlook the fact that it is hard to find someone that you can trust. Not only did the companions begin to leave, but many also seemed to encounter extremely bad luck.

After the deal, material wealth seemed to come fast but, also the realization that the more you have, the more you must keep up with and, the older you get the less you feel like it. No matter how much power you have, all your material wealth can do is get you in trouble and destroy your peace. The dealer finds that he needs help from others (he certainly cannot manage all the material wealth alone), but it is hard to find those who can be trusted. The most heart-breaking reality is, too much time has passed much too fast. In the end, there is the reality that no wealth or power can defeat "old age".

Eventually, you begin to see that you have lost something. No matter what you want people to see, all they really see is an old person. Someone who has lived their life and should be retiring and leaving the world to the young so that they can live theirs. The feeling of satisfaction that is supposed to be there is not there and there is no happy place to return to. While the dealer has been haunting fortune and fame old age and death have been haunting him and now there is no escape. Each day that goes by finds that there are so many new things happening that people are less interested in him.

An old man speaking about how great he is, cannot compete with youth and it's much easier to say how great you are than it is to prove it. It would seem more reasonable to want fewer stresses in life as we grow older. The thing about selling one soul is that once you enter a deal, there is no way out. You began to find out you're not nearly as clever as you thought. The tools that Satan provided, that worked so well before are seeming to make the dealer a laughingstock now. Those who attempt to help him seem less wise.

The person who once thought that he was smarter than the devil himself, now wonders where he went wrong. He wonders when he changed from someone who had all the answers for himself and everyone else, to someone needing help, support and money from his followers. A deal with the devil changed a man who could fix anything, who had everything and didn't need anything to a person crying; "Look what they are doing to me. Now I must face the consequences of my actions when I should be retired, resting and doing fun things. Now, I don't even have a soul to sell."

THE END